Kate
the Royal Wedding Fairy

Daisy Meadows

ORCHARD

www.rainbowmagic.co.uk

The Fairyland Palace

Chapel

Royal Workshop

Spiral Tower

Crypt

Jack Frost's
Ice
Castle

Throne
Room

Contents

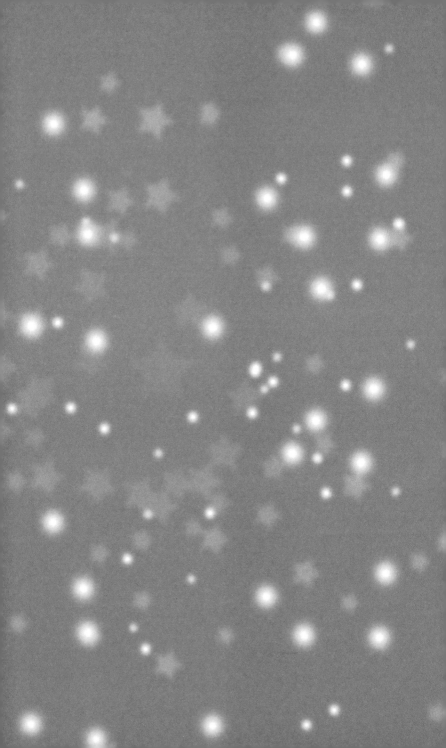

Story One

A Very Special Adventure

Chapter One

A Flowery Friend

It was a lovely spring day in Tippington. Kirsty Tate was spending half term with her best friend, Rachel Walker. They had been roller-skating in the park all morning!

As they walked along the path, Rachel suddenly stopped.

"What's the matter?" asked Kirsty.

Rachel pointed at the flowerbeds.

"Look at that rose!" she said in a hushed voice.

All the other flowers were swaying in the spring breeze, but one deep-red rose wasn't moving.

"It's glowing!" Rachel cried. "Oh, Kirsty, I think something magical is about to happen."

The two best friends knew a lot about magic.

Ever since they had first met, they had enjoyed a secret friendship with the Rainbow Magic fairies. They'd had lots of wonderful adventures in Fairyland!

Rachel and Kirsty stared at the rose as its petals opened slowly. They saw a tiny fairy inside! She had lovely shiny brown hair topped by a sparkly tiara.

She was wearing a gown of ivory silk, and a gold pendant hung around her neck.

"Hello, Rachel and Kirsty," she said in a silvery voice. "I'm Kate the Royal Wedding Fairy. I make sure that royal weddings go well in Fairyland and the human world!"

"It's wonderful to meet you!" Kirsty replied with a big smile.

"I'm so pleased to see you both," said Kate. "The fairies need your help! Please will you come to Fairyland at once?"

"Of course!" chorused
Rachel and Kirsty.
The girls both knew that
time would stand still in the
human world while they were
in Fairyland.

Kate
smiled
and
waved
her
wand.
Tiny

glittering pink roses and red
heart shapes surrounded the
girls. Rachel and Kirsty both felt
themselves shrinking to fairy size
as they were lifted into the air
and carried to the centre of the
rose. Floaty wings appeared on
their backs.

Kate waved her wand again, and shimmering golden sparkles spun around the girls. They were off to Fairyland!

Chapter Two

Magical Fairyland!

In no time at all, the three
friends were flying above the
glimmering Fairyland Palace.
Kirsty and Rachel spotted lots
of their old fairy friends! The
Petal Fairies were decorating
the palace door with garlands
of white and pink flowers.

"There is going to be a very special wedding here this afternoon," Kate explained. "Princess Grace is getting married to Prince Arthur!

She is King Oberon and Queen Titania's niece."

Kate led the girls through the garden to the Seeing Pool. She explained that Queen Titania was going to meet them there.

"How will your magic help the royal wedding go well?" asked Rachel.

"I am in charge of the True Love Crown," replied Kate with a smile. "Its magic is very special indeed. It makes sure that the royal couple will live happily ever after.

Princess Grace has to wear the True Love Crown when she says her marriage vows."

"That sounds so magical!" said Kirsty with a sigh, as the three friends arrived at the Seeing Pool.

Kate nodded. "The crown is very precious," she said. "It's always safely locked up in the Spiral Tower, watched over carefully by the frog guards. But yesterday, the True Love Crown was taken out of the tower to be polished.

As the guard was carrying
the crown to the palace,
something terrible happened."

Kate's voice trembled slightly,
and she paused.

Rachel exchanged a serious
glance with Kirsty. What was
Kate going to tell them…?

Chapter Three

The Goblinovski Ballet

"I will show you what happened," said a kind voice.

The girls whirled around and saw Queen Titania standing there. They curtseyed as she walked towards them.

"Thank you both for coming," said the queen.

"We know we can always
depend on your help!"

The queen waved her wand
over the Seeing Pool. A picture
appeared in the sparkling water.
"Look, there's Bertram the
frog footman!" cried Rachel.

Bertram was a friend of theirs.

In the picture they saw
Bertram handing a young
frog guard a red velvet cushion.
On the cushion was a beautiful
golden crown, sparkling with
bright jewels.

"Stanley, take the crown
to the palace to be polished,"
Bertram said.

Stanley nodded solemnly
and left the tower. But as he
walked past the green, he
spotted a very strange group
of dancers prancing about!

They were wearing sparkly tights and feathery hair decorations.

Stanley stood and stared in astonishment as the dancers took their positions.

"The Goblinovski Festival Ballet presents 'A Spring Surprise'," cried the plumpest dancer, and the group began to bounce, hop and twirl around!

It was the strangest dance routine that Rachel or Kirsty had ever seen. Stanley stood watching with his mouth hanging open in astonishment.

"I am proud to introduce the most amazing dancer in the whole world," announced another dancer. "Here's FROSTYEV!"

A dancer with a spiky silver tutu and a large feathery head-dress appeared and danced crazily across the green towards the other dancers.

Finally, Frostyev and the dancers finished. Stanley put the cushion down on the ground in front of him and clapped politely. But when he looked down, he gave a cry of horror. Instead of the True Love Crown, there was a large cabbage sitting on the red velvet cushion!

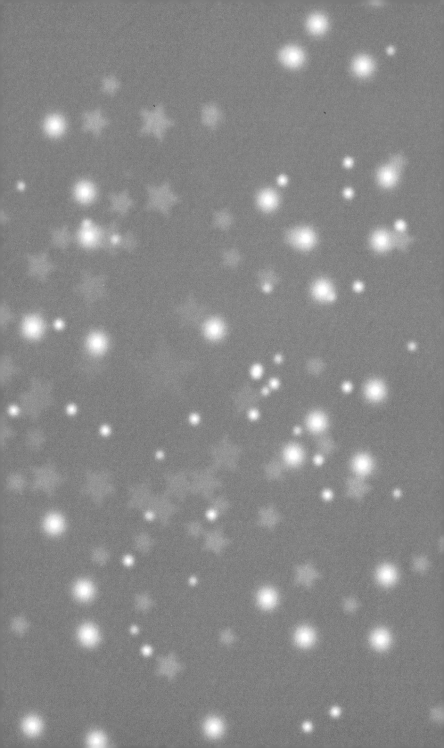

Story Two
The True Love Crown

Chapter One

Frost Thieves

Poor Stanley the frog footman couldn't believe that the True Love Crown had been stolen. "Stop, thieves!" he cried.

Frostyev ripped off his tutu and head-dress. Rachel and Kirsty gasped in horror.

"It's Jack Frost!" cried Kirsty.

Rachel looked more closely at the dancers.

"They all have enormous feet!" she exclaimed. "And I can see green skin through their costumes. Oh, Kirsty, they're goblins!"

Jack Frost created an ice bolt for each of the goblin dancers.

Then he held up the True Love
Crown for everyone to see.

"Those pesky fairies will
never get their silly crown
back!" he gloated. With their
ice bolts, he and his goblin
gang shot off into the sky.

The picture in the Seeing

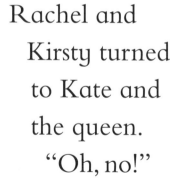

Pool faded and
Rachel and
Kirsty turned
to Kate and
the queen.

"Oh, no!"
said Rachel.

"We have to get the True Love Crown back or Princess Grace and her new husband won't live happily ever after!"

Kirsty and Rachel knew that Jack Frost would have taken the crown to his Ice Castle. The girls had visited his home before. It was a dark and scary place!

Kirsty, Rachel and Kate went to the palace to prepare for their journey to the Ice Castle. They saw one fairy flying towards the palace kitchens, with the ingredients for a cake.

Another was sitting in the palace library, writing a spell to make sure that the sun would shine brightly on the bride and groom all day long!

"I've never seen the palace so full of fairies," Rachel said.

"But they all look sad. On a special day like this, they should be full of happiness and excitement."

"Then we just have to get the True Love Crown back," said Kirsty. "Let's make sure Princess Grace and Prince Arthur are happy forever, and make our fairy friends joyful again!"

Chapter Two

To the Ice Castle

Rachel, Kirsty and Kate flew as fast as they could towards the Ice Castle. They soon entered Jack Frost's icy realm and saw his home looming ahead of them.

The three friends zoomed around the castle wall, keeping a look out for goblin guards.

Kate suddenly stopped beside a tall window.

"Listen!" she said in a whisper. "I can hear Jack Frost!"

"That's the Throne Room," said Kirsty, moving nearer. "And look – the window is open!"

They slipped into the Throne Room and hid behind the curtains hanging in the window.

Jack Frost was sitting on his throne. In front of him, a plump goblin was holding up a cushion. On the cushion was the magnificent True Love Crown.

"There it is!" said Rachel.

"We must get it back," Kate whispered. "Princess Grace's happiness depends on us."

But Jack Frost grabbed the cushion and put it on his lap. "Look at my beautiful sparkly crown!" he chuckled. "It's going to make me look even more handsome than I already am!"

"What if the king and queen come looking for it?" asked the plump goblin.

"Ha!" screeched Jack Frost. "They already have a crown each – they don't need this one!"

Just then, three goblins dashed up to the throne carrying a large piece of cloth.

It looked like a very old, dirty
tablecloth.

"Your cloak is ready," one
goblin said.

"About time!" exclaimed Jack
Frost, leaping off his throne
and placing it around his
shoulders. They all looked at it.

It was made
of worn bits
of cloth,
dirty dusters
and smelly
old socks!

"It's perfect,"
said Jack Frost. "A wonderful
match for my splendid new
crown. This will be the best
coronation the Ice Castle has
ever seen!"

Chapter Three

A Castle Coronation

As soon as Jack Frost said
'coronation', Kate gave a groan.

"What's wrong?" asked Kirsty.

"And what is a 'coronation'?"
wondered Rachel aloud.

"It is a royal ceremony
that makes someone a king
or queen," Kate explained.

"And the True Love Crown's magic is activated by these royal ceremonies. So, even though this won't be a real coronation, the power of the True Love Crown means that

 as soon as Jack Frost puts it on his head, he will fall completely in love with the first person he sees!"

Kirsty and Rachel both gasped in horror.

Jack grabbed one of his goblin servants by the shoulder.

"For my special coronation, I need an official companion," he said.

The goblin grumbled under his breath, but he lined up with the other green rascals behind a tall goblin in a pointy ceremonial hat. Jack Frost walked beside his companion goblin. A goblin at the back carried the True Love Crown. The fairies flitted after them, staying out of sight.

The group wound down crumbling old steps to a cold, dark room.

The tall goblin wearing the hat stood on a raised block of stone and faced his master and the other goblins.

"We are gathered here today to witness the coronation of Jack Frost," said the goblin, his hat falling over his eyes.

"This might be our best chance to get the crown," Kate whispered.

"We'll have to be very quick to take it before they can catch us," Rachel whispered back. "Come on!"

Everyone was looking at Jack Frost. Kate, Rachel and Kirsty swooped down towards the True Love Crown. But just as they reached it, Jack Frost spun around.

"Pesky fairies!" he shouted.

Jack Frost raised his wand.

He blasted the three fairies
with a bolt of icy magic. Then
he hissed a spell, and spiky
rocks shot down from the
ceiling, freezing into a
large icy cage all around them.

The friends gasped in horror. They were trapped! How on Earth would they rescue the True Love Crown now?

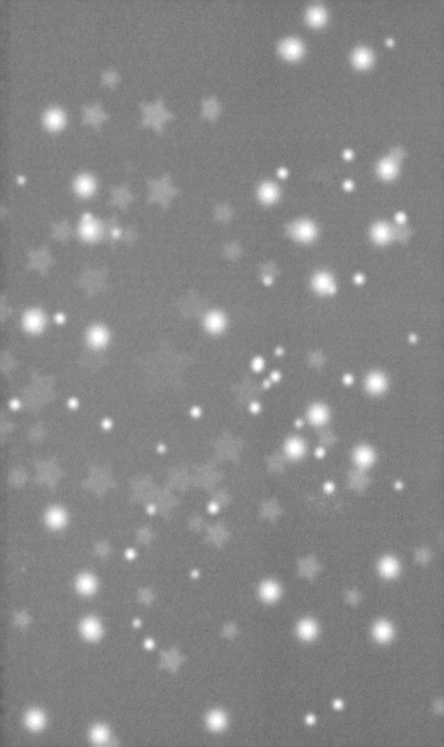

Story Three

The Royal Wedding

Chapter One

Jack Frost in Love!

Trapped in their icy prison, Kirsty, Rachel and Kate had to watch Jack Frost's silly coronation ceremony unfold before their very eyes. First, the tall goblin unfurled a large scroll of paper and began to read aloud.

"Do you, Jack Frost, promise to rule your goblins with unfair treatment and general meanness?"

"I do," said Jack Frost solemnly.

"Will he fall in love for ever with the first person he sees?" whispered Rachel, as the tall goblin asked Jack Frost more silly questions.

"No," Kate told her. "Because this isn't a real ceremony, the True Love Crown's special magic won't work like that.

It will only work while Jack is actually wearing the crown!"

Just then the plump goblin clambered awkwardly onto the shoulders of another goblin,

and held the crown above Jack
Frost's head.

"I pronounce Jack Frost
Master of Goblins and
ruler of the
world!" cried the
tall goblin.

The girls held
their breath as the
True Love Crown was lowered
onto Jack Frost's spiky head. As
it touched him, he was glaring
at the goblin. A glow came from
the crown, and the girls saw
Jack Frost's expression change.

A soppy smile spread across his face and the Ice Lord stroked the goblin's green head lovingly.

"Oh!" he declared, dropping to his knees. "Was there ever a goblin more beautiful than you?"

The other goblins were all staring open-mouthed. They could hardly believe their ears!

"Give me a cuddle!" pleaded Jack Frost, drawing the horrified goblin towards him.

"NOOOO!" squawked the goblin, trying to get away. "I'm scared!"

In the struggle, the crown toppled from Jack Frost's head onto the ground and the enchantment was broken. With a shriek, Jack Frost picked up the True Love Crown and threw it at Kate, Kirsty and Rachel. "This crown is cursed!" he yelled.

The girls gasped as the crown spun through the air and crashed into their rocky prison, smashing it to bits.

Kate grabbed the crown as it fell, and straight away it returned to fairy size.

Then, before the goblins could move, she grabbed her wand and used her fairy magic to whisk herself, Rachel and Kirsty straight back to the Fairyland Palace!

Chapter Two

A Truly Magical Wedding

Kate, Rachel and Kirsty arrived outside the palace and saw Princess Grace with Mia the Bridesmaid Fairy, waiting for her coach to take them to the palace chapel. The three friends smiled. They were just in time for the wedding!

Two gleaming white unicorns trotted around the corner, pulling a sparkling glass coach behind them.

As Princess Grace and Mia the Bridesmaid Fairy climbed into the coach, Kate led Rachel and Kirsty over to the palace chapel. She waved her wand over both of them, and their everyday clothes were transformed into beautiful dresses!

"Thank you so much!" breathed Kirsty and Rachel.

Kate led them up the aisle to
the front row, beside Queen
Titania. When the queen saw
the crown, she smiled at them.

"My dears," she said. "Once
again you have saved us all."

Suddenly there was a commotion at the back of the chapel. Jack Frost and his goblins had walked in!

"Don't worry," smiled the queen. "They were invited to the wedding."

Rachel and Kirsty settled in the front row as Jack Frost stood nearby, with his arms crossed. He was still looking very grumpy.

"Lovey-dovey nonsense,"

the girls heard him muttering under his breath.

Just then, the Music Fairies began to play the Wedding March. Everyone stood up as the bride walked up the aisle.

The prince's eyes sparkled with love as he looked at her.

Kate placed the True Love Crown on the bride's head, then the king performed the ceremony. As the happy couple said their vows, sparkling fairy dust flowed from the crown, and encircled both of them. The magic was working!

As the king pronounced them husband and wife, the chapel rang with fairy cheers. The Rainbow Fairies' special wedding rainbow arched over the bride and groom, and joyful music filled the air.

"Thank you all," said Princess Grace. "Now, I would like to invite everyone to the palace ballroom for a grand party!"

Chapter Three

Happily Ever After

Kirsty and Rachel didn't
think that there had ever been
such a wonderful party in the
history of Fairyland! There
was a spectacular feast, the
Music Fairies played enchanted
melodies and Cherry the Cake
Fairy had baked a lovely cake.

It was
frosted
with pink
icing and
decorated
with
sugared
roses.

There
were dazzling displays from
the Dance Fairies and show-
stopping performances from the
Showtime Fairies. Even Jack
Frost jumped up for a dance
with his goblins!

"The bride and groom look so happy," said Kirsty.

Princess Grace and Prince Arthur were waltzing in the centre of the ballroom, surrounded by the magical glow from the True Love Crown.

"Their love will last for ever," said Kate with a soft smile.

Afterwards, everyone gathered outside the palace under the silvery stars. Then the night sky was lit up by a magical fireworks display!

When the display finished,

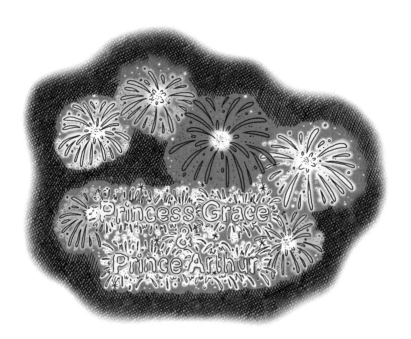

the pink glow of dawn was on
the horizon.

Rachel sighed. "We should be
going home."

Kate gave them both a huge
hug. "Thanks to you, the prince
and princess are starting their
lives together with happiness,"

she said. "That is the most wonderful gift anyone could give them!"

"Thank you for letting us help," said Kirsty. "A royal fairy wedding is the best celebration in the world!"

The girls held hands and waved goodbye to their fairy friends. Streams of glittering fairy dust surrounded them. Rachel and Kirsty closed their eyes, and when they opened them again they were standing by the flowerbeds in Tippington Park.

Kirsty noticed that two red roses were nodding in their direction. "Rachel, look!" she said.

They bent down, and as they got closer, the flowers opened. In the centre of each rose was a tiny pink flower corsage brooch. Attached to them was a note.

These corsages will never
fade, and will keep their
scent for ever.
With love,
Kate the Royal
Wedding Fairy.

Rachel and Kirsty pinned
the corsages on each other.
The sweet smell of fresh roses
wafted up to them.

"What an amazing
adventure," Rachel smiled at
her best friend.

Kirsty nodded in agreement.

"It was truly magical. Long live the prince and princess!"

The End

**If you enjoyed this story,
you may want to read**

Georgie the
Royal Prince Fairy
Early Reader

Here's how the story begins…

"Rachel, are you awake?"
whispered Kirsty Tate.

It was an early Saturday
morning in Wetherbury, Kirsty's
home town, but this was not an
ordinary weekend.

"Yes, I've been awake for

hours. I'm too excited to sleep!" Rachel Walker replied. "Can you believe we're going to see three real princes today?"

"And we're actually going to meet them at the palace garden party tomorrow," added Kirsty with a happy sigh. "It's like a dream, isn't it?"

Read
Georgie the Royal Prince Fairy Early Reader

to find out
what happens next!